THE HAT-SHAKING DANCE

by Harold Courlander

Folk Tales

THE HAT-SHAKING DANCE (Ghana)

THE TIGER'S WHISKER
(Asia and the Pacific)

KANTCHIL'S LIME PIT (Indonesia)

THE COW-TAIL SWITCH
(West Africa)
with George Herzog

THE FIRE ON THE MOUNTAIN
(Ethiopia) with Wolf Leslau

TERRAPIN'S POT OF SENSE
(United States)

THE KING'S DRUM
(Africa south of the Sahara)

RIDE WITH THE SUN
(around the world)

UNCLE BOUQUI OF HAITI (Haiti)

THE PIECE OF FIRE (Haiti)

Other

THE DRUM AND THE HOE—Life and Lore of the Haitian People

THE BIG OLD WORLD OF RICHARD CREEKS

THE CABALLERO

NEGRO FOLK MUSIC U. S. A.

SHAPING OUR TIMES—What the United Nations Is and Does

HAITI SINGING

ON RECOGNIZING THE HUMAN SPECIES

NEGRO SONGS FROM ALABAMA

The Hat-Shaking Dance

And Other Ashanti Tales from Ghana

by Harold Courlander

with Albert Kofi Prempeh

Illustrated by Enrico Arno

Harcourt, Brace & World, Inc., New York

For Erika, Michael, and Susan

Contents

The Ashanti,
from whom these stories come...

North of the Gulf of Guinea, in the country of Ghana,
live the people known as the Ashanti. Where they originally came from is not clear, but it is believed that long
ago they migrated to this land from somewhere farther
north.

The Ashanti built a civilization in this land. They had
their poets, their singers, their historians, their music, their
dancing, their festivals, and their gods. They carefully
preserved their legends which told of the ancient migra-
tions of their ancestors, of the deeds of heroes, of how
the world began, and how certain customs came to be.
They had complex laws and rules of behavior, some of
them strange to Europeans, but adapted to the needs of
their own way of life. They had concepts of right and
wrong which were not greatly different from those of
other peoples of the world. Honor and truth were
revered. Dishonor and treachery were despised.

The Ashanti knew the life of the towns and the clear-
ings; they knew also the deep forest which stood like a
great wall behind them. They cleared and planted the
earth, and they hunted wild game of the forest. There

were fine artists and craftsmen among them—weavers, metalsmiths, wood carvers, and drum makers. They had good lawgivers and bad, warlike men and peaceful men, ruthless men and kind men. Like people everywhere, they possessed both superstition and wisdom.

Today life among the Ashanti is changing, as life everywhere is changing. The King of Ashanti, the Asantehene, lives in a modern house and performs his work in an office.

But the old traditions are not forgotten. In the Ashanti villages at night, children gather to hear stories which contemplate on right and wrong, or stories of justice and injustice, or tales that simply make them laugh. Many tales are about the spider, known as Anansi. He is at the same time the shrewdest and most stupid of all creatures, sometimes a hero and sometimes a scoundrel. All tales are called Anansesem, in honor of Anansi, for he is their owner. And this is how such a strange thing came to be . . .

THE HAT-SHAKING DANCE

ll Stories Are Anansi's

In the beginning, all tales and stories belonged to Nyame, the Sky God. But Kwaku Anansi, the spider, yearned to be the owner of all the stories known in the world, and he went to Nyame and offered to buy them.

The Sky God said: "I am willing to sell the stories, but the price is high. Many people have come to me offering to buy, but the price was too high for them. Rich and powerful families have not been able to pay. Do you think you can do it?"

Anansi replied to the Sky God: "I can do it. What is the price?"

"My price is three things," the Sky God said. "I must first have Mmoboro, the hornets. I must then have Onini, the great python. I must then have Osebo, the leopard. For these things I will sell you the right to tell all stories."

Anansi said: "I will bring them."

He went home and made his plans. He first cut a gourd from a vine and made a small hole in it. He took a large calabash and filled it with water. He went to the tree where the hornets lived. He poured some of the water over himself, so that he was dripping. He threw some water over the hornets, so that they too were dripping. Then he put the calabash on his head, as though to protect himself from a storm, and called out to the hornets: "Are you foolish people? Why do you stay in the rain that is falling?"

The hornets answered: "Where shall we go?"

"Go here, in this dry gourd," Anansi told them.

The hornets thanked him and flew into the gourd through the small hole. When the last of them had entered, Anansi plugged the hole with a ball of grass, saying: "Oh, yes, but you are really foolish people!"

He took his gourd full of hornets to Nyame, the Sky God. The Sky God accepted them. He said: "There are two more things."

Anansi returned to the forest and cut a long bamboo pole and some strong vines. Then he walked toward the house of Onini, the python, talking to himself. He said: "My wife is stupid. I say he is longer and stronger. My wife says he is shorter and weaker. I give him more respect. She gives him less respect. Is she right or am I right? I am right, he is longer. I am right, he is stronger."

When Onini, the python, heard Anansi talking to himself, he said: "Why are you arguing this way with yourself?"

The spider replied: "Ah, I have had a dispute with my wife. She says you are shorter and weaker than this bamboo pole. I say you are longer and stronger."

Onini said: "It's useless and silly to argue when you can find out the truth. Bring the pole and we will measure."

So Anansi laid the pole on the ground, and the python came and stretched himself out beside it.

"You seem a little short," Anansi said.

The python stretched further.

"A little more," Anansi said.

"I can stretch no more," Onini said.

"When you stretch at one end, you get shorter at the other end," Anansi said. "Let me tie you at the front so you don't slip."

He tied Onini's head to the pole. Then he went to the other end and tied the tail to the pole. He wrapped the vine all around Onini, until the python couldn't move.

"Onini," Anansi said, "it turns out that my wife was right and I was wrong. You are shorter than the pole and weaker. My opinion wasn't as good as my wife's. But you were even more foolish than I, and you are now my prisoner."

Anansi carried the python to Nyame, the Sky God,

who said: "There is one thing more."

Osebo, the leopard, was next. Anansi went into the forest and dug a deep pit where the leopard was accustomed to walk. He covered it with small branches and leaves and put dust on it, so that it was impossible to tell where the pit was. Anansi went away and hid. When Osebo came prowling in the black of night, he stepped into the trap Anansi had prepared and fell to the bottom. Anansi heard the sound of the leopard falling, and he said: "Ah, Osebo, you are half-foolish!"

When morning came, Anansi went to the pit and saw the leopard there.

"Osebo," he asked, "what are you doing in this hole?"

"I have fallen into a trap," Osebo said. "Help me out."

"I would gladly help you," Anansi said. "But I'm

sure that if I bring you out, I will have no thanks for it. You will get hungry, and later on you will be wanting to eat me and my children."

"I swear it won't happen!" Osebo said.

"Very well. Since you swear it, I will take you out," Anansi said.

He bent a tall green tree toward the ground, so that its top was over the pit, and he tied it that way. Then he tied a rope to the top of the tree and dropped the other end of it into the pit.

"Tie this to your tail," he said.

Osebo tied the rope to his tail.

"Is it well tied?" Anansi asked.

"Yes, it is well tied," the leopard said.

"In that case," Anansi said, "you are not merely half-foolish, you are all-foolish."

And he took his knife and cut the other rope, the one that held the tree bowed to the ground. The tree

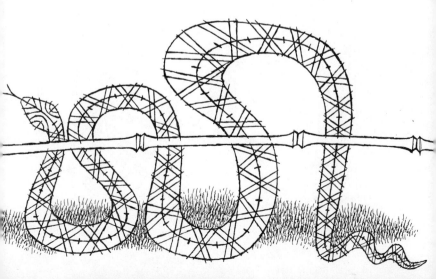

straightened up with a snap, pulling Osebo out of the hole. He hung in the air head downward, twisting and turning. And while he hung this way, Anansi killed him with his weapons.

Then he took the body of the leopard and carried it to Nyame, the Sky God, saying: "Here is the third thing. Now I have paid the price."

Nyame said to him: "Kwaku Anansi, great warriors and chiefs have tried, but they have been unable to do it. You have done it. Therefore, I will give you the stories. From this day onward, all stories belong to you. Whenever a man tells a story, he must acknowledge that it is Anansi's tale."

In this way Anansi, the spider, became the owner of all stories that are told. To Anansi all these tales belong.

Anansi, the Oldest of Animals

It happened one time that the animals of the fields and the forest had a great argument about which of them was the oldest and entitled to the most respect. Each of them said: "I am the oldest." They argued at great length, and at last they decided to take the case before a judge. They went to the house of Anansi, the spider, and they said to him: "Kwaku Anansi, we are in dispute as to which of us is the most venerable. Listen to our testimony."

So Anansi called his children to bring him a cashew shell, and he sat on it with great dignity, as though he were a chief sitting on a carved stool.

The guinea fowl was the first to speak. He said: "I swear it. I am the oldest of all creatures. When I was born, there was a great grass fire. Since there was no one else in the world to put it out, I ran into the flames and stamped them out with my feet. My legs were badly burned, and as you can see, they are still red."

The animals looked at the guinea fowl's legs and saw it was true: they were red. They said: "Eeee! He is old!"

Then the parrot declared:

"I swear it. When I came into the world, there were no tools and no weapons. It was I who made the first hammer that was ever used by blacksmiths. I beat the iron into shape with my beak, and it is for this reason that my beak is bent."

The animals looked at the parrot's beak, crying out: "Eeee! The parrot is old indeed!"

Then the elephant spoke:

"I swear it. I am older than the parrot and the guinea

fowl. When I was created, the Sky God gave me a long and useful nose. When the other animals were made, there was a shortage of material, and they were given small noses."

The animals examined the elephant's nose and shouted: "Eeeeee! The elephant is truly old!"

The rabbit gave his testimony then, saying:

"I swear it. I am the oldest. When I came into the world, night and day had not yet been created."

The animals applauded the rabbit. They said: "Eeeeee! Is he not really the oldest?"

The porcupine spoke last, and he said:

"I swear it. As you will all have to admit, I am the

oldest. When I was born, the earth wasn't finished yet. It was soft like butter and couldn't be walked upon."

This was great testimony, and the animals cheered the porcupine. They cried: "Eeeeee! Who can be older than he?"

Then they waited to hear Anansi's judgment. He sat on his cashew shell and shook his head, saying:

"If you had come to me first, I would have saved you this argument, for I am the oldest of all creatures. When I was born, the earth itself had not yet been made, and there was nothing to stand on. When my father died, there was no ground to bury him in. So I had to bury him in my head."

And when the animals heard this they declared:

"Eeeeee! Kwaku Anansi is the oldest of all living things! How can we doubt it?"

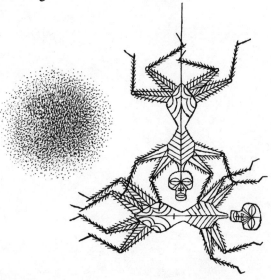

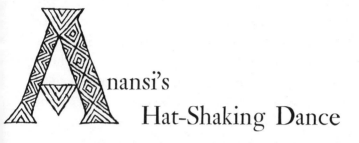

Anansi's Hat-Shaking Dance

If you look closely, you will see that Kwaku Anansi, the spider, has a bald head. It is said that in the old days he had hair, but that he lost it through vanity.

It happened that Anansi's mother-in-law died. When word came to Anansi's house, Aso, his wife, prepared to go at once to her own village for the funeral. But Anansi said to Aso: "You go ahead; I will follow."

When Aso had gone, Anansi said to himself: "When I go to my dead mother-in-law's house, I will have to show great grief over her death. I will have to refuse to eat. Therefore, I shall eat now." And so he sat in his own house and ate a huge meal. Then he put on his mourning clothes and went to Aso's village.

First there was the funeral. Afterwards there was a large feast. But Anansi refused to eat, out of respect for his wife's dead mother. He said: "What kind of man would I be to eat when I am mourning for my mother-in-law? I will eat only after the eighth day has passed."

Now this was not expected of him, because a man isn't required to starve himself simply because someone has died. But Anansi was the kind of person that when he ate, he ate twice as much as others, and when he danced, he danced more vigorously than others, and when he mourned, he had to mourn more loudly than anybody else. Whatever he did, he didn't want to be outdone by anyone else. And although he was very hungry, he couldn't bear to have people think he wasn't the greatest mourner at his own mother-in-law's funeral.

So he said: "Feed my friends, but as for me, I shall do without." So everyone ate—the porcupine, the rabbit, the snake, the guinea fowl, and the others. All except Anansi.

On the second day after the funeral they said to him again: "Eat, there is no need to starve."

But Anansi replied: "Oh no, not until the eighth· day, when the mourning is over. What kind of man do you think I am?"

So the others ate. Anansi's stomach was empty, and he was unhappy.

On the third day they said again: "Eat, Kwaku Anansi, there is no need to go hungry."

But Anansi was stubborn. He said: "How can I eat when my wife's mother has been buried only three days?" And so the others ate, while Anansi smelled the food hungrily and suffered.

On the fourth day, Anansi was alone where a pot of beans was cooking over the fire. He smelled the beans and looked in the pot. At last he couldn't stand it any longer. He took a large spoon and dipped up a large portion of the beans, thinking to take it to a quiet place and eat it without anyone's knowing. But just then the dog, the guinea fowl, the rabbit, and the others returned to the place where the food was cooking.

To hide the beans, Anansi quickly poured them in his hat and put it on his head. The other people came to the pot and ate, saying again: "Anansi, you must eat."

He said: "No, what kind of man would I be?"

But the hot beans were burning his head. He jiggled his hat around with his hands. When he saw the others looking at him, he said: "Just at this very moment in my village the hat-shaking festival is taking place. I shake my hat in honor of the occasion."

The beans felt hotter than ever, and he jiggled his hat some more. He began to jump with pain, and he said: "Like this in my village they are doing the hat-shaking dance."

He danced about, jiggling his hat because of the heat. He yearned to take off his hat, but he could not because his friends would see the beans. So he shouted: "They are shaking and jiggling the hats in my village, like this! It is a great festival! I must go!"

They said to him: "Kwaku Anansi, eat something before you go."

But now Anansi was jumping and writhing with the heat of the beans on his head. He shouted: "Oh no, they are shaking hats, they are wriggling hats and jumping like this! I must go to my village! They need me!"

He rushed out of the house, jumping and pushing his hat back and forth. His friends followed after him saying: "Eat before you go on your journey!"

But Anansi shouted: "What kind of man do you think I am, with my mother-in-law just buried?"

Even though they all followed right after him, he couldn't wait any longer, because the pain was too

much, and he tore the hat from his head. When the dog saw, and the guinea fowl saw, and the rabbit saw, and all the others saw what was in the hat, and saw the hot beans sticking to Anansi's head, they stopped chasing him. They began to laugh and jeer.

Anansi was overcome with shame. He leaped into the tall grass, saying: "Hide me." And the grass hid him.

That is why Anansi is often found in the tall grass, where he was driven by shame. And you will see that his head is bald, for the hot beans he put in his hat burned off his hair.

All this happened because he tried to impress people at his mother-in-law's funeral.

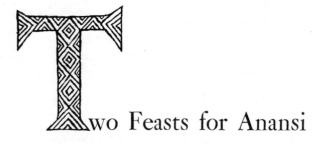

Two Feasts for Anansi

Kwaku Anansi's thin belly came from greed. It is said that one year there was a wedding feast in the town of Kibbes, and another wedding feast in the town of Diabee, and they were both on the same day. Anansi asked himself: "Which feast will I go to?" He thought, and then he said: "I am very hungry. I will go to both. I will eat first at the place where the food is served first, and afterwards I will go to the other place and eat again."

But Anansi couldn't find out which of the feasts would come first. He went to Diabee and asked: "When will the food be served?" But they couldn't tell him. So he went then to the town of Kibbes and asked: "What time will the food be given out?" But they didn't know. He went back and forth between the two towns, first the one and then the other, until he was weary. But still he knew nothing about where the food would be given out first.

So Kwaku Anansi bought two long ropes, and he sent for his sons Intikuma and Kweku Tsin. He tied both ropes around his middle. He gave the end of one rope to Intikuma, saying: "Take this end of the rope with you and go to Diabee. When they start giving out the food, pull hard on the rope and I will come." He gave the end of the other rope to Kweku Tsin, saying: "Take this with you to Kibbes. When the feast begins, pull hard and I will come. This way I will know where the food is given out first."

So Intikuma went to Diabee, taking the end of one rope with him, and Kweku Tsin went to Kibbes, taking the end of the other rope with him. Each of them stood in the town and waited to give the signal.

But when the feasts began in Diabee and Kibbes, they began at the very same moment. Intikuma pulled and Kweku Tsin pulled. As they both pulled very hard, Anansi couldn't go one way or another. He was halfway between, and he couldn't move. His sons pulled harder and harder, and they didn't stop until the feasts were ended and the food was gone. Then they went to see what had detained their father.

They found him where they had left him, but he didn't look the same. Where the ropes had squeezed him around the middle he had become very small. And this way he has always remained. The spider carries with him forever the mark of his greed.

Anansi Plays Dead

One year there was a famine in the land. But Anansi and his wife Aso and his sons had a farm, and there was food enough for all of them. Still the thought of famine throughout the country made Anansi hungry. He began to plot how he could have the best part of the crops for himself. He devised a clever scheme.

One day he told his wife that he was not feeling well and that he was going to see a sorcerer. He went away and didn't return until night. Then he announced that he had received very bad news. The sorcerer had informed him, he said, that he was about to die. Also, Anansi said, the sorcerer had prescribed that he was to be buried at the far end of the farm, next to the yam patch. When they heard this news, Aso, Kweku Tsin, and Intikuma were very sad. But Anansi had more instructions. Aso was to place in his coffin a pestle and mortar, dishes, spoons, and cooking pots, so that Anansi could take care of himself in the Other World,

In a few days, Anansi lay on his sleeping mat as though he were sick, and in a short time he pretended to be dead. So Aso had him buried at the far end of the farm, next to the yam patch, and they put in his coffin all of the cooking pots and other things he had asked for.

But Anansi stayed in the grave only while the sun shone. As soon as it grew dark, he came out of the coffin and dug up some yams and cooked them. He ate until he was stuffed. Then he returned to his place in the coffin. Every night he came out to select the best part of the crops and eat them, and during the day he hid in his grave.

Aso and her sons began to observe that their best yams and corn and cassava were being stolen from the fields. So they went to Anansi's grave and held a special service there. They asked Anansi's soul to protect the farm from thieves.

That night Anansi again came out, and once more he took the best crops and ate them. When Aso and her sons found out that Anansi's soul was not protecting them, they devised a plan to catch the person who was stealing their food. They made a figure out of sticky gum. It looked like a man. They set it up in the yam patch.

That night Anansi crawled out of his coffin to eat.

He saw the figure standing there in the moonlight.

"Why are you standing in my fields?" Anansi said.

The gum-man didn't answer.

"If you don't get out of my fields, I will give you a thrashing," Anansi said.

The gum-man was silent.

"If you don't go quickly, I will have to beat you," Anansi said.

There was no reply. The gum-man just stood there. Anansi lost his temper. He gave the gum-man a hard blow with his right hand. It stuck fast to the gum-man. Anansi couldn't take it away.

"Let go of my right hand," Anansi said. "You are making me angry!"

But the gum-man didn't let go.

"Perhaps you don't know my strength," Anansi

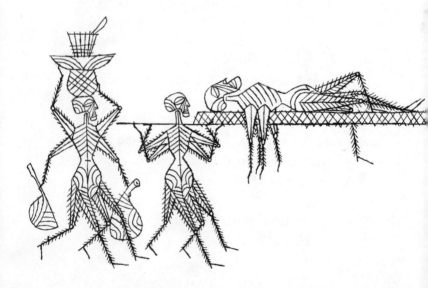

said fiercely. "There is more power in my left hand than in my right. Do you want to try it?"

As there was no response from the gum-man, Anansi struck him with his left hand. Now both his hands were stuck

"You miserable creature," Anansi said, "so you don't listen to me! Let go at once and get out of my fields or I will really give you something to remember! Have you ever heard of my right foot?"

There was no sound from the gum-man, so Anansi gave him a kick with his right foot. It, too, stuck.

"Oh, you like it, do you?" Anansi shouted. "Then try this one, too!"

He gave a tremendous kick with his left foot, and now he was stuck by both hands and both feet.

"Oh, are you the stubborn kind?" Anansi cried. "Have you ever heard of my head?"

And he butted the gum-man with his head, and that stuck as well.

"I'm giving you your last chance now," Anansi said sternly. "If you leave quietly, I won't complain to the chief. If you don't, I'll give you a squeeze you will remember!"

The gum-man was still silent. So Anansi took a deep breath and gave a mighty squeeze. Now he was completely stuck. He couldn't move this way or that. He couldn't move at all.

In the morning when Aso, Kweku Tsin, and Intikuma came out to the fields, they found Anansi stuck helplessly to the gum-man. They understood everything. They took him off the gum-man and led him toward the village to be judged by the chief. People came to the edge of the trail and saw Anansi all stuck up with gum. They laughed and jeered and sang songs about him. He was deeply shamed, and covered his face with his headcloth. And when Aso, Kweku Tsin, and Intikuma stopped at a spring to drink, Anansi broke away and fled. He ran into the nearest house, crawled into the rafters, and hid in the darkest corner he could find.

From that day until now, Anansi has not wanted to face people because of their scoffing and jeering, and that is why he is often found hiding in dark corners.

The Liars' Contest

One day the fly, the moth, and the mosquito went hunting together. They came upon Anansi in the forest. "There is meat," they said, and they seized Anansi, and there was a struggle. But Anansi was stronger than he looked, and they were unable to overcome him. At last they stopped to rest.

Anansi asked: "Why are you hunting me?"

They replied: "We are hungry. As you know, all living things must eat."

Anansi said: "I also must eat. Why shouldn't I eat you?"

"You aren't strong enough to subdue us," they said.

"Nor are you strong enough to subdue me," Anansi said. "Let us make a bargain. You may tell me a fantastic story. If I say I don't believe it, you may eat me. I will tell you a story. If you say it isn't true, I will eat you."

The three hunters agreed. So the moth told his story first.

"Before I was born," the moth said, "my father settled on new land, but that very day he cut his foot with a bush knife and couldn't work. So I jumped up and cleared away the forest, cultivated the ground, planted it with corn, weeded it, harvested the corn, and put it in the granary. When I was finally born a few days later, my father was already a rich man."

The moth, the fly, and the mosquito looked at Anansi, waiting for him to say, "I do not believe it," so that they could eat him. But Anansi said: "How truly you have spoken! How true it is!"

Then the mosquito told his story. He said:

"When I was only four years old, I was sitting peacefully in the forest chewing on an elephant that I had killed. But I felt like playing, and when I saw a leopard slink by, I chased him. When I was just about to catch him, he turned around and opened his jaws to swallow me. I quickly stuck my hand down his throat and seized the inside of his tail. Then I gave it a quick pull and turned the leopard inside out. The leopard had eaten a sheep. And now the sheep was on the outside and the leopard was inside. The sheep thanked me properly and grazed off into the grass."

The mosquito, the fly, and the moth waited for Anansi to say, "That is a lie," so they could begin eating him. But Anansi said: "Oh, how true! How true!"

So then the fly had his turn. He said:

"This is my story. I went hunting in the forest one day and tracked down an antelope. I aimed my gun at him, fired, then ran forward and caught the antelope, turned him on his side, skinned him, and cut the meat into quarters. Just then the bullet which I had fired came along. I caught it and replaced it in my gun. I was hungry, so I carried the meat to the top of a tall tree, built a fire on a limb, and cooked a meal. I ate the entire antelope. When it was time to come down, I had eaten so much that my stomach was swollen, and I was too heavy to climb. So I went back to the village and got a rope. Then I returned to the tree, tied the rope around my waist, and let myself carefully down to the ground."

The fly, the moth, and the mosquito waited quietly for Anansi to say, "Oh, what an impossibility," but instead of that he said: "This is a true tale of true tales!"

Now it was Anansi's turn.

"Last year I planted a coconut tree," Anansi said. "One month later it was grown. I was hungry, so I cut three coconuts down. I opened the first nut with my bush knife, and a fly came out. I opened the second one, and a moth came out. I opened the third one, and a mosquito came out. As I had planted the tree on which they were grown, the fly and the moth and the mosquito belonged to me. But when I tried to eat them, they ran away. I have been searching for them

ever since so that I could eat them. And now at last I have found you—my fly, my mosquito, and my moth."

The three hunters were silent.

Anansi asked: "Haven't you anything to say?"

They wanted to say, as Anansi had said, "How true, how true!" But they dared not, because then Anansi would claim them as his lost property and eat them. And they could not say he had lied, because then they would lose the contest, and Anansi would eat them. They couldn't make up their minds whether to cry truth or falsehood. At last they simply turned and fled.

And ever since then, whenever Anansi, the spider, catches flies, moths, or mosquitoes, he eats them, because he outwitted them in the lying contest.

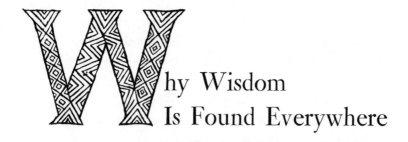

hy Wisdom Is Found Everywhere

Kwaku Anansi regarded himself as the wisest of all creatures. He knew how to build bridges, to make dams and roads, to weave, and to hunt. But he didn't wish to share this wisdom with other creatures. He decided one day that he would gather together all the wisdom of the world and keep it for himself. So he went around collecting wisdom, and each bit he found he put in a large earthen pot. When the pot was full, Anansi prepared to carry it into a high treetop where no one else could find it. He held the pot in front of him and began to climb.

Anansi's son Intikuma was curious about what his father was doing, and he watched from behind some bushes. He saw Anansi holding the pot in front of him against his stomach. He saw that this made it hard for Anansi to grasp the tree he was climbing. At last he couldn't keep quiet any longer and he said: "Father, may I make a suggestion?"

Anansi was startled and angry, and he shouted: "Why are you spying on me?"

Intikuma replied: "I only wanted to help you."

Anansi said: "Is this your affair?"

Intikuma said to him: "It's only that I see you are having difficulty. When you climb a tree, it is very hard to hold a pot in front. If you put the pot on your back, you can climb easily."

Anansi tried it. He took the pot from in front and put it on his back. He climbed swiftly. But then he stopped. He looked at Intikuma and was embarrassed, for although he carried so much wisdom in the pot, he had not known how to climb with it.

In anger, Kwaku Anansi took the pot and threw it from the treetop. It fell on the earth and shattered into many pieces. The wisdom that was in it scattered in all directions. When people heard what had happened, they came and took some of the wisdom Anansi had thrown away. And so today, wisdom is not all in one place. It is everywhere. Should you find a foolish man, he is one who didn't come when the others did to take a share of the wisdom.

This is the story the Ashanti people are thinking of when they say: "One head can't exchange ideas with itself."

sebo's Drum

Osebo, the leopard, once had a great drum which was admired by all animals and gods. Although everyone admired it, no one ever hoped to own it, for Osebo was then the most powerful of animals on earth, and he was feared. Only Nyame, the Sky God, had ambitions to get the drum from the leopard.

It happened one time that Nyame's mother died, and he began the preparations for a spectacular funeral. He wondered what he could do to make the ceremony worthy of his family. People said to him: "For this ceremony we need the great drum of Osebo."

And Nyame said: "Yes, I need the drum of Osebo."

But Nyame didn't know how he could get the drum. At last he called the earth animals before him, all but the leopard himself. Nyame's stool was brought out, and he sat upon it, while his servants held over his head the many-colored parasol which is called the rainbow. He said to the animals:

"For the funeral ceremonies I need the great drum of the leopard. Who will get it for me?"

Esono, the elephant, said: "I will get it." He went to where the leopard lived and tried to take the drum, but the leopard drove him away. The elephant came back to the house of the Sky God, saying: "I could not get it."

Then Gyata, the lion, said: "I will get the drum." He went to the place of the leopard and tried to take the drum, but the leopard drove him off. And Gyata, the lion, returned to the house of the Sky God, saying: "I could not get it."

Adowa, the antelope, went, but he couldn't get it. Odenkyem, the crocodile, went, but he couldn't get it. Owea, the tree bear, went, but he couldn't get it. Many animals went, but the leopard drove them all away.

Then Akykyigie, the turtle, came forward. In those days the turtle had a soft back like other animals. He said to the Sky God: "I will get the drum."

When people heard this, they broke into a laugh, not even bothering to cover their mouths. "If the strong creatures could not get Osebo's drum," they said, "how will you, who are so pitifully small and weak?"

The turtle said: "No one else has been able to bring it. How can I look more foolish than the rest of you?"

And he went down from the Sky God's house, slowly, slowly, until he came to the place of the leopard. When Osebo saw him coming, he cried out: "Are you too a messenger from Nyame?"

The turtle replied: "No, I come out of curiosity. I want to see if it is true."

The leopard said: "What are you looking for?"

"Nyame, the Sky God, has built himself a great new drum," the turtle said. "It is so large that he can enter into it and be completely hidden. People say his drum is greater than yours."

Osebo answered: "There is no drum greater than mine."

Akykyigie, the turtle, looked at Osebo's drum, saying: "I see it, I see it, but it is not so large as

Nyame's. Surely it isn't large enough to crawl into."

Osebo said angrily: "Why is it not large enough?" And to show the turtle, Osebo crawled into the drum.

The turtle said: "It is large indeed, but your hind quarters are showing."

The leopard squeezed further into the drum.

The turtle said: "Oh, but your tail is showing."

The leopard pulled himself further into the drum. Only the tip of his tail was out.

"Ah," the turtle said, "a little more and you will win!"

The leopard wriggled and pulled in the end of his tail.

Then the turtle plugged the opening of the drum with an iron cooking pot. And while the leopard cried out fiercely, the turtle tied the drum to himself and began dragging it slowly, slowly, to the house of Nyame, the Sky God. He dragged for a while; then he stopped to beat the drum as a signal that he was coming.

When the animals heard the great drum of Osebo, they trembled in fear, for they thought surely it was Osebo himself who was playing. But when they saw the turtle coming, slowly, slowly, dragging the great drum behind him, they were amazed.

The turtle came before the Sky God and said: "Here is the drum. I have brought it. And inside the drum is Osebo himself. What shall I do with him?"

Inside the drum Osebo heard, and he feared for his life. He said: "Let me out, and I will go away in peace."

The turtle said: "Shall I kill him?"

The animals all said: "Yes, kill him!"

But Osebo called out: "Do not kill me; allow me to go away. The drum is for the Sky God, and I won't complain."

So the turtle removed the iron pot which covered the opening in the drum. Osebo came out frightened. He came hurriedly. And he came out backwards, tail first. Because he couldn't see where he was going, he fell into the Sky God's fire, and his hide was burned in many little places by the hot embers. He leaped from the fire and hurried away. But the marks of the fire, where he was burned, still remain, and that is why all leopards have dark spots.

The Sky God said to the turtle: "You have brought the great drum of Osebo to make music for the funeral of my mother. What can I give you in return?"

The turtle looked at all the other animals. He saw that they were jealous of his great deed. And he feared that they would try to abuse him for doing what they could not do. So he said to Nyame: "Of all things that could be, I want a hard cover the most."

So the Sky God gave the turtle a hard shell to wear on his back. And never is the turtle seen without it.

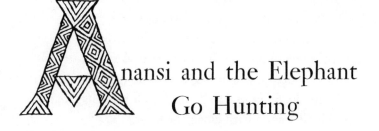

Anansi and the Elephant Go Hunting

It is said that once in the old days there was a famine in the world and that Anansi schemed to get meat to eat. His wife, Aso, said: "Find us yams."

But Anansi replied: "Where will I find yams, for the earth is dried up, and there are no yams."

Aso asked him then: "Wherever will you find meat?"

And Anansi said: "I have a plan."

He went to the place where the elephant lived, and he invited the elephant to go foraging with him for food. Esono, the elephant, agreed, and the two of them went into the forest together. Esono said to Anansi: "Wherever shall we find yams? The earth is dried up, and there are no yams in this country."

Anansi replied: "I know a place where there are fine yams. There is a huge garden deep in the forest. I go there whenever there is a famine and take all the

38

yams I can carry."

Esono, the elephant, said: "I never heard of this wonderful place. You lead the way, and I will follow."

So Anansi led the elephant among the big trees of the forest. They went further and further, until there was no longer a path. Anansi moved easily through the dense forest, for he was small, but the elephant was big, and he walked with difficulty. It was dark among the great trees, and the elephant couldn't see very well. He called out to Anansi: "Are you there?"

Anansi replied: "I am here; follow me."

Then at last Anansi led the elephant between two great trees which stood close together. In those days Esono, the elephant, was even larger behind than he was in front, and he found himself wedged between the trees.

"I cannot move," Esono said.

Anansi said: "Push harder."

The elephant tried to force himself between the trees, but the harder he pushed, the tighter he was stuck. At last he said: "I cannot move."

"If you stay this way, you will be food for the leopard," Anansi said.

"How can I avoid it?" the elephant asked.

Anansi said: "Let us rest. I will think."

So Anansi rested and thought, but what he thought was what he had been thinking before they went into the great forest. At last he spoke.

"If I could cut away a little of the meat behind

you," Anansi said, "you would be small enough to pass through the trees."

The elephant said: "Cut, cut, there is no other way!"

Anansi answered him: "If you wish it." He took his knife and cut large portions of meat from the elephant's hips, until the elephant became small enough behind to pass through the trees where he had been caught.

Anansi said to him: "Wait here and I will return." But he didn't return. He took the meat and went out of the forest. He came to his house, announcing: "Here is meat." Then he locked the door, and they cooked and ate elephant meat.

Esono, the elephant, waited a long time for Anansi to return. Finally he went home by himself. When he arrived at his house, his family cried out: "What has happened to you? You have changed. Once you were large behind; now you are small!"

Esono turned and looked at himself. When he saw what had happened, he became angry. He cried out to his youngest son: "Anansi has stolen my meat! Go to his house and reclaim it!"

So the elephant child went to Anansi's house. When Anansi heard him coming, he gave a drum to his son Intikuma and commanded him to beat it just so—*katapkatap! rotototo! katapkatap!* Intikuma beat it just so — *katapkatap! rotototo! katapkatap!* And Anansi sang:

> "*Who stands on the threshold?*
> *Who stands on the threshold?*
> *Why are you standing when you should*
>   *be dancing?*"

The elephant child replied, singing the same tune:

> "*I am the youngest son of the elephant!*
> *I am the youngest son of the elephant!*
> *I am here to take back my father's meat!*"

Then Anansi replied, singing:

> "*We have tasted the meat; it is good!*
> *We have tasted the meat; it is good!*
> *Why are you standing when you should*
>   *be dancing?*"

And now the elephant child couldn't keep his feet still any longer, for the music was making him dance. He danced all around the house, backwards and forwards, around and around, and he couldn't stop.

Esono, the elephant, waited a long time for his youngest son to return. At last he sent his second son. When the second son arrived, he saw his brother dancing. He heard the drum going *katapkatap! rotototo! katapkatap!* And he heard Anansi singing:

> "*Who stands on the threshold?*
> *Who stands on the threshold?*
> *Why are you standing when you should*
>   *be dancing?*"

The elephant child answered:

> "*I am the second son of Esono!*
> *I am the second son of Esono!*
> *I am here to take back my father's meat!*"

And Anansi sang:

> "*We have tasted the meat; it is good!*
> *We have tasted the meat; it is good!*
> *Why are you standing when you should*
>   *be dancing?*"

The drum went *katapkatap*, and the elephant child went *katapkatap* with his feet. The drum went *rotototo*, and the elephant child went *rotototo* with

his feet. He could not stand still any longer, and soon he was dancing with his brother. The two of them were dancing back and forth, here and there. They couldn't stop.

After a while Esono, the elephant, sent his eldest son to reclaim the meat. The eldest son heard the music first; then he saw his brothers dancing. And before he was able to accomplish his business with Anansi, he, too, was dancing, up and down, around and around, this way and that way.

Esono waited. When none of his sons returned, he was truly angry, and he himself went to Anansi's house to reclaim his meat. When he arrived, he saw his children dancing a wild dance, and he heard Anansi's

drum going *katapkatap! rotototo! katapkatap!* He shouted to his sons to stop, but they couldn't stop. He beat on Anansi's door, and Anansi sang:

> *"Who stands on the threshold?*
> *Who stands on the threshold?*
> *Why are you standing when you should*
>   *be dancing?"*

Esono, the elephant, shouted angrily:

> *"I am Esono, the son of my father!*
> *I am Esono, the son of my father!*
> *I am here to take back my meat!"*

Anansi sang back:

> *"We have tasted the meat; it is good!*
> *We have tasted the meat; it is good!*
> *Why are you standing when you should*
>   *be dancing?"*

And suddenly Esono, too, began to dance. He couldn't help it. His feet just moved of their own accord in time to the drum. He danced, danced, danced. Back and forth, around the house, forwards and backwards and sidewards. He stamped here and there and raised a cloud of dust from the stamping. He trampled down the fences. He danced a deep pit in the courtyard.

"Stop the drumming!" he shouted. "I can't dance any more!" But the drum went on, *katapkatap! rotototo! katapkatap!* At last Esono called out:

"Stop the music and I'll go away. As for the meat, it

no longer matters. We will say that you have bought the meat and paid for it with this dance! And I will say no more about it!"

So Anansi stopped the music. Esono and his children stopped dancing, and they went away wearily. And that was how it happened that the elephant's hind parts became smaller than his foreparts. And ever since, the elephant has avoided the forests where he was tricked by Anansi. Instead, he lives now in the tall grass country.

The Planting Party

A farmer one day prepared to plant a field of corn. As was the custom, he started out to invite his neighbors to come and help him with the planting. The corn seed spoke, saying: "Whatever you do, don't invite the termite, for when the termite sees corn, he can't resist eating it."

But the farmer paid no attention. He went to the termite and asked him to join the work party. The termite said: "I will be glad to help, but whatever you do, don't invite the chicken. It is hard for a chicken and a termite to work together without the chicken's getting ideas."

Nevertheless, the farmer went next to the chicken and asked him to help. "Certainly I will come," the chicken said, "but please don't invite the snake."

The farmer went then to the snake and asked, and the snake agreed. But he said: "Whatever you do, don't invite the stick."

The farmer went to the stick's house, saying: "Please come to help in the corn planting." The stick answered: "Naturally I will come. But don't invite the fire."

The farmer then invited the fire to help. The fire replied: "I will be there. But whatever you do, don't invite water."

The farmer went to water's house. The water agreed to join the party, but he said: "Promise not to invite the sun."

However, the farmer needed the sun. He went to the sun's house and asked him, too. And the sun agreed to be there.

The planting day arrived, and all of the farmer's neighbors were on the field. The corn seed turned his head and saw the termite. The termite turned his head and saw the chicken. The chicken turned his head and saw the snake. The snake turned his head and saw the stick. The stick turned and saw the fire. The fire turned and saw the water. The water turned and saw the sun. All the enemies were together on the field.

They began to hoe up the earth. Suddenly the termite turned and accused the corn of insulting him.

The corn replied: "But I haven't said a word."

The termite said: "When you argue with me, you know what happens to you!" And he caught hold of the corn and swallowed it.

Then the chicken said to the termite: "Why have

you done this to the corn?" And without waiting for an answer, the chicken swallowed the termite.

The snake said to the chicken: "Why have you done this offensive thing to the helpless termite?" And he swallowed the chicken.

The stick then admonished the snake, saying: "What have you done to the kind chicken?" He struck the snake and killed him.

The fire reproached the stick for killing the snake, and he caught the stick and burned it up.

The water was angered by this. It threw itself on the fire and put it out.

Then the sun began to shine hotly, and the water dried up and disappeared.

Just at this moment the praying mantis came along and saw all the desolation. Everything was chaos and destruction. The praying mantis was overcome with awe and dismay. He slapped both hands against his sides, exclaiming: "Wye!" But he slapped too hard. He slapped so hard that he became very thin in the middle. And that is the way he remains to this day.

Okraman's Medicine

Okraman, the dog, had a hunger that he couldn't control. Whenever he found food, he ate it if he could. Sometimes the food was his; sometimes it belonged to others; but it made no difference. When he was hungry, he couldn't tell what food was his and what food wasn't his. And because he had a reputation for stealing food, he couldn't find a wife in his village. No one wanted to be related to him.

So Okraman went to a distant town where they didn't know him, and there he found a wife. He brought her back to his village, and they lived there. Then one day his wife went back to her own town to visit her parents. After a while Okraman was lonesome, and he sent a message to his wife that he also would come to visit her parents.

When the message came, the girl's father took his weapons and went into the forest to get meat, so that there could be a feast in honor of Okraman. He killed an antelope. He brought it to the house, prepared it, and put it over a fire in the courtyard to cook.

Okraman arrived. He saw the meat cooking. His mouth watered. When night came, everyone went into the house to sleep. But Okraman couldn't sleep. He smelled the antelope cooking over the fire. He got up from his sleeping mat to go out and look at the meat. He saw the fat dripping into the fire. He went back to his mat and lay down. He got up and went out again to look at the meat. He went back to his sleeping mat and closed his eyes. He got up once more to go and look at the cooking meat. He licked a little of the dripping fat. He nibbled a little of the meat, gently, with his front teeth. He couldn't stop chewing. He swallowed a little. He swallowed more. He couldn't stop chewing until the meat was all gone. Only then did he go back and lie down on his mat. He slept.

When morning came, Okraman's wife went out to sweep up the courtyard. She saw that the antelope meat was gone. She cried out: "The meat has been eaten! The meat has been eaten!" Okraman awoke. He heard the people talking. He was overcome with shame that he had eaten the meat his father-in-law had hunted for a feast in his honor. He covered his face with a cloth so that no one would see his shame, and he fled from the town.

He arrived in his own village. His friends said: "What are you doing here? We thought you were feasting at the house of your father-in-law."

Okraman replied: "I went, but I couldn't stay. Last night I got up and ate the meat my father-in-law hunted in my honor. I am shamed. Now I am looking for someone with powerful medicine to cure me of thieving."

The people said: "Go see Adanko, the hare. He has powerful medicine for such things."

The dog went to the hare's house. He said: "Adanko, help me. I am a thief. I cannot help stealing meat when I see it. They say you have powerful medicine. Cure me. Whatever it costs, I will pay it."

Adanko said: "I can cure you of stealing. I need only the meat of a wild pig for the medicine."

So Okraman went hunting and killed a wild pig, which he brought to the hare. The hare cut off a portion of the meat and put it over the fire to cook. He took spices and leaves and rubbed them into the meat. He rubbed peppers and onions into it. It cooked. The dog watched it cooking. He heard it sizzle. He smelled it.

When night came, the hare said: "Okraman, go into the house and sleep. When morning comes, I will take the meat from the fire and make powerful medicine with it that will cure you forever of thieving."

Okraman went to his mat to sleep. Adanko went to his mat to sleep. Adanko slept. Okraman didn't sleep. He smelled the meat. He heard it sputtering over the fire. At last he woke the hare, saying: "Father Adanko,

Father Adanko! There are mice in the village. They will eat the meat. I will protect it. I will bring it and put it beside me."

Adanko replied: "Do it then. I don't care as long as I have the meat tomorrow to make the medicine."

So the dog went out and took the meat. He brought it in and put it next to his mat. But he couldn't sleep. He called out to the hare: "Father Adanko! The mice are in the house. I had better put the meat under my pillow."

Adanko said: "Why do you wake me? Do it then, as long as I have it tomorrow to make the medicine."

Okraman put the meat under his pillow. He closed his eyes and made sleeping sounds with his nose. But

he couldn't sleep. He smelled the meat under the pillow. Again he called out, waking the hare: "Father Adanko, Father Adanko! The mice are under the pillow! I will take the meat and place it on my head, and I will stand here until morning!"

The hare replied: "Stand, then, and place the meat on your head. What do I care, as long as the meat is here when day comes!"

Okraman stood up. He took the meat and placed it on top of his head. And there he stood. But a little of the juice trickled down his face and into his mouth. He licked it. He called out to Adanko urgently: "Father Adanko! I think the mice are on my head! I think I had better hold the meat in my mouth!"

Adanko was angered to be awakened again. He said: "Hold it in your mouth then!"

Okraman put the meat in his mouth. He held it there grimly. He walked around and around the room groaning, his tail wagging, going this way and that way. At last he called out frantically: "Oh, Father Adanko, let me owe you for this meat!"

The hare said: "No, no! The meat is for the medicine to cure you of your thieving."

But Okraman's agony was too great. He let some of the meat go down his throat. He let more go down, until finally there was nothing left in his mouth at all. Then he went to his mat and truly slept.

When daylight came, the hare arose, saying: "Where now is the meat? I will prepare the medicine."

Okraman said: "Oh, Father Adanko, I told you last night I would have to owe you for it."

The hare asked: "Why should you owe me for it?"

And Okraman replied: "Because last night the mice came into my teeth, and I had to swallow the meat to save it."

Then the hare said: "As you have eaten the meat, Okraman, I cannot make medicine to cure you. Therefore, as long as he lives, the dog will steal food and eat it."

And so he does.

Anansi Borrows Money

It happened once that Anansi, the spider, needed money. He went to his neighbors for help, but Anansi's reputation wasn't good, and no one would lend him anything. He went to the leopard and the bush cow, but they refused him. He went to the guinea fowl, the turtle, and the hawk, but they all refused him. Then he went to a distant village where Owoh, the snake, lived. Owoh lent him the money he needed, on condition that it would be returned by the end of twenty-one days.

But when twenty-one days had passed, Anansi had no money to repay the loan. He began to think of ways to get out of his predicament. He went to his garden and dug up a basket full of yams. He put the basket on his head and carried it to the house of Owoh, the snake.

He said to Owoh: "This is the day I was to repay

the money you so kindly lent me. But there is a small complication. I won't have the money for two or three days yet, and I hope you will be kind enough to wait. In the meanwhile, I have brought some yams to share with you in gratitude for your help."

Anansi used many sweetened words, and the snake agreed to wait three more days for his money. Of the yams he had brought, Anansi gave half to the snake. Owoh shared his portion with his friends. Anansi kept his portion in the basket. Owoh treated Anansi with great hospitality and invited him to stay overnight in his house. So Anansi stayed.

But in the middle of the night Anansi arose from his sleeping mat quietly and went out. He took the yams he had saved for himself away from the house. He took them out into the bush and hid them in the ground. When he returned, he placed his empty basket in front of the house and went back to sleep.

In the morning he came out and said to Owoh: "Where are my yams?" But Owoh knew nothing about the yams. So Anansi took his empty basket and returned home. He went to the headman of the district to make a complaint that his yams had been stolen. The people of the district were very concerned. They said to each other: "What kind of a thief is it who would steal yams from someone who has been as generous as Anansi?"

The headman called for a trial to find the guilty person. The people of all the villages came. Anansi said to them:

"There is only one test to prove innocence. I have a magic knife. I will draw it across the skin of each person. It will not cut those who are innocent of this crime. It will cut only those who are guilty."

Then each of the animals came forward for the test. When the guinea fowl came, Anansi drew his knife across the guinea fowl's skin, but he used the blunt edge instead of the sharp edge. He did the same with the turtle, the rabbit, and the other animals. No one was hurt. When the snake's turn came, he said: "Test me."

But Anansi refused, saying: "Oh no. It is unthinkable that you who have been so good as to lend me money would steal my yams." But Owoh insisted, saying: "I also must have my turn. You were in my house when the yams were stolen. All the others have taken the test. I, too, must prove my innocence." Anansi protested that it was unnecessary, and Owoh protested that he must be cleared of any suspicion of guilt.

"Very well," Anansi said at last. "Since it is your wish, I will let you take the test."

So Anansi drew his knife across the skin of Owoh, but this time he used not the blunt edge but the sharpened edge, and he killed him. The people said: "He has failed the test; he must be guilty!"

As Owoh died, however, he rolled on his back,

turning his belly to the sky, as if to say: "Oh God, look at my belly and see whether I have eaten Anansi's yams!"

It is for this reason that whenever a snake is killed, he turns his belly to the sky, calling upon God to judge his innocence.

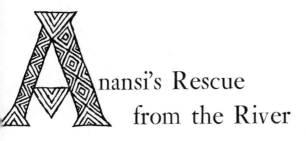

Anansi's Rescue from the River

When the first of Anansi's sons was born, Anansi prepared to give him a name. But the baby spoke up and said: "You needn't bother to name me. I have brought my own name. I am called Akakai." This name signified "Able to See Trouble."

When the second of Anansi's sons was born, he too announced that he had brought his own name. "I am called Twa Akwan," he said. This name signified "Road Builder."

When the third son was born, he said: "My name is Hwe Nsuo." That meant "Able to Dry Up Rivers."

When the fourth was born, he announced: "I am Adwafo." That meant "The Skinner of Game."

The fifth son said when he was born: "I have been named already. I am known as Toto Abuo." His name signified "Stone Thrower."

The sixth son told Anansi: "I am called Da Yi Ya." That meant "Lie on the Ground Like a Cushion."

Intikuma and Kweku Tsin had not yet been born, so Anansi had in those days only six sons in all.

One day Kwaku Anansi went on a long journey. Several weeks passed, and he failed to return. Akakai, the son who had the ability to see trouble, announced that Anansi had fallen into a distant river in the middle of a dense jungle.

Twa Akwan, the builder of roads, constructed a highway through the jungle, and the brothers passed through it to the edge of the river.

Hwe Nsuo, who had the power to dry up rivers, dried up the river, and they found there a great fish which had swallowed Anansi.

Adwafo, the skinner of game, cut into the fish and

released his father.

But as soon as they brought Anansi to the edge of the river, a large hawk swooped down out of the sky, caught Anansi in his mouth, and soared into the air with him.

Toto Abuo, the stone thrower, threw a rock into the sky and hit the hawk, which let go of Anansi.

And as Anansi dropped toward the earth, Da Yi Ya threw himself on the ground like a cushion to soften his father's fall.

Thus Kwaku Anansi was saved by his six sons and brought home to his village.

Then one day when he was in the forest, Anansi found a bright and beautiful object called Moon.

Nothing like it had ever been seen before. It was the most magnificent object he had ever seen. He resolved to give it to one of his children.

He sent a message to Nyame, the Sky God, telling him about his discovery. He asked Nyame to come and hold the Moon, and to award it as a prize to one of Anansi's sons—the one who had done the most to rescue him when he was lost in the river.

The Sky God came and held the Moon. Anansi sent for his sons. When they saw the Moon, each of them wanted it. They argued. The one who had located Anansi in the jungle river said he deserved the prize. The one who had built the road said he deserved it. The one who had dried up the river said he deserved it. The one who had cut Anansi out of the fish said he deserved it. The one who had hit the hawk with the stone said he deserved it. The one who had cushioned Anansi's fall to earth said he deserved it.

They argued back and forth, and no one listened to anybody else. The argument went on and on and became a violent squabble. Nyame, the Sky God, didn't know who should have the prize. He listened to the arguments for a long time. Then he became impatient. He got up from where he sat and went back to the sky, taking the Moon along with him.

And that is why the Moon is always seen in the heavens, where Nyame took it, and not on the earth where Anansi found it.

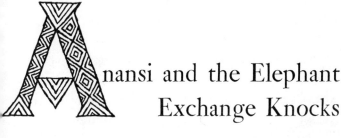

Anansi and the Elephant Exchange Knocks

Anansi was walking in the bush one day when he saw Esono, the elephant, playing by himself. Esono was testing his strength by pulling up trees by the roots and throwing them into the air. This display of strength annoyed Anansi. So he insulted Esono by saying: "Who is this childish creature who is pulling out shoots of grass?"

The elephant looked around, surprised. He had a hard time locating Anansi. When he saw him at last, he said: "Are you speaking to me?"

Anansi said: "Yes, you silly grass-puller, I am talking to you."

The elephant was annoyed by the insult. He said: "Are you tired of life? If I should step on you, there would be nothing left but your name."

"Very well," Anansi said with dignity, "let us wrestle to test our strength."

When the elephant heard this, he laughed. He said: "What could be more ridiculous!"

"Very well then," Anansi said, "let us exchange knocks."

The elephant thought it was very funny, but he accepted the challenge. It was agreed that the elephant would give the first knocks. He would have three tries. Then it would be Anansi's turn, and he, too, would have three tries. Three nights Esono would come to Anansi's house to give him knocks, and three nights Anansi would go to Esono's house to return the knocks.

All the way home Anansi was thinking what he would do, for he knew he would never be able to survive a single knock from the elephant. Then he worked out a plan. He would have to have someone else take his knocks for him.

It happened that yams were very scarce in the country that year. He went home and filled a basket with yams and carried it down to the river. He waited until he saw Adanko, the hare, coming. Then he began to throw the yams into the river, saying: "This will give me more room; this will give me more room."

The hare looked in amazement. He said: "Anansi, what are you doing, throwing yams in the river when there is a famine in the country?"

Anansi replied: "Oh, it's no matter. I have so many yams I don't have room to keep them. Why don't you come to my house and help me eat them?"

The hare said: "Do you mean it?"

And Anansi replied: "Positively."

So the hare came to Anansi's house, and they cooked some yams and ate them. Afterwards, Anansi asked Adanko to stay and help him receive the yams.

"What do you mean, receive the yams?" Adanko asked.

"Oh, every night a servant comes to the window and brings another load," Anansi said. "Be a good friend and receive them for me. When he says: 'Are you ready to take it?' you say to him, 'Yes, I am ready.' That is all."

"Then I will do it," the hare said, and he stayed.

Anansi went to sleep, while Adanko stood at the window. In the dark of night the elephant came. He

said: "Are you ready to take it?"

Adanko, the hare, replied: "Yes, give it to me."

The elephant gave it to him. He gave him a terrific blow with his trunk and went away. The hare was finished.

The next day Anansi went again to the river with a basket of yams. When he saw the guinea fowl coming, he began to throw yams into the river, saying: "Now there'll be more room; now there'll be more room."

The guinea fowl cried out: "Anansi, what are you doing, throwing yams away in a time of famine?"

"Oh, I have so many," Anansi said. "They are crowding me out of my house. Please come and help me eat them."

"Do you mean it?" the guinea fowl asked.

"Positively," Anansi said.

So the guinea fowl came and ate, and when it was time to sleep, Anansi said: "Friend, help me receive the yams tonight."

The guinea fowl said: "What shall I do?"

"Stand at the window," Anansi said. "When my servant comes, he will ask: 'Are you ready?' Simply say you are ready, and he will give it to you."

So the guinea fowl stood at the window while Anansi slept. The elephant came in the darkness, and he said: "Are you ready to take it on your head?"

"I am ready," the guinea fowl replied. "Give it to me."

The elephant gave it to him. He gave him a mighty knock with his trunk. The guinea fowl was finished.

The next day Anansi went to the river again with yams. He threw them into the water, saying: "Now I'll have more room; now I'll have more room." This time he surprised Kotoko, the porcupine, and brought him home with him. He instructed Kotoko the same way as he had the guinea fowl and the hare.

Kotoko stood at the window. The elephant came and said: "Are you ready for more?"

The porcupine said: "Yes, give it to me." And then the porcupine was finished.

Now it was Anansi's turn to give the knocks. He went to the blacksmith and bought a heavy hammer.

Then he went to the elephant's house in the dark of night, saying: "Here I am. Are you ready?"

The elephant said: "Yes, of course."

Anansi hit him with the hammer.

"Oh!" the elephant said in amazement. The blow hurt him. "Oh! Can Anansi be as strong as that?"

The next night Anansi came again. He said: "Are you ready for the second blow?"

"Oh," the elephant said, remembering the first one, "oh, I think so...."

Anansi gave him another knock with the hammer. This time the elephant cried out in pain.

Again, the third night, Anansi came and called out: "Esono! Are you ready for the third blow? Tonight I am really going to give it to you!"

"I am here," Esono said weakly.

"Are you ready?"

"I think so ... I don't know ... Yes ... Maybe ..." the elephant said. And then, remembering the two blows he had already received, the elephant suddenly roared out in panic: "Run for your lives! Anansi is here giving out blows!"

Esono's family began to run. They fled in all directions. Some went east, some west, some south, and some north. Some went into the mountains, some went into the plains, and some went to distant lands.

And this is why there now are elephants everywhere.

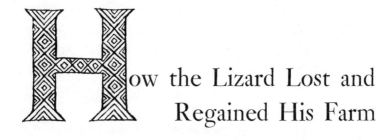

ow the Lizard Lost and Regained His Farm

It was a time of famine, and Kwaku Anansi was wondering how he would be able to fill his storehouse with food. He heard from his son Intikuma that Abosom, the lizard, had a fine garden, so he went to see for himself. As Intikuma had described it, so it was. The lizard's garden was green and flourishing. Anansi said to himself: "If I had this garden, I'd have no more worries." So he went home and planned how to get it from the lizard.

One night when Abosom's crop was ready for harvesting, Anansi collected all his children together, saying: "Follow me and do whatever I do." He walked from the doorway of his house to the lizard's garden, the children walking behind him. Then he turned and walked back to his doorway. He walked back to lizard's place. Then he walked back to his house. The children began to complain, asking whether Anansi couldn't make up his mind. But he said angrily: "Don't question your elders! Follow me and do as I do!"

Back and forth they went. All night they marched. When the sun began to return and things became visible, they saw that where they had been marching there was now a trail, where formerly there had been only tall grass. Then Anansi gave his children baskets and digging knives, and they began to dig up the yams and harvest the other crops on the lizard's land.

When lizard came, he saw Anansi's family taking all his crops, and he cried out: "What are you doing on my land?"

Anansi replied: "Your land? It is my land. And why do you stand there in my garden without asking my permission?"

They argued this way for a long while, until the lizard said: "We shall go to the chief of the district and ask for a judgment."

They went to the chief and presented their cases. First Anansi said: "It is my land." Then Abosom said: "It is my land." And each one gave his reasons.

The chief listened. At last he went to the garden to see for himself. He said to Abosom: "Where is your house?" The lizard showed him his house. The chief then asked him: "Where is the path from your house?" The lizard was surprised at such a question. He answered: "There is no path. Among my people, when we go from one place to another, we rarely go

71

twice the same way. Sometimes we go on top of the grass. Sometimes we go between the grass. Sometimes we jump from tree to tree."

When the chief heard this, he shook his head. "This is unheard of," he said. "Whenever someone goes from somewhere that is his to something that is his, he makes a path." Then the chief turned to Anansi, asking: "Where is your path?" And Anansi showed him.

"This is my judgment," the chief declared. "As Anansi has a path from his house to the garden, the garden is his."

When the lizard heard this, he lost the power of words. He could not say anything, because the judgment had been so false. He simply moved his head up and down without making a sound, calling on the Sky God Nyame to witness his misfortune.

The chief went home, and the lizard went home. As for Anansi, he and his children carried away all the food and put it in their storehouse.

But the lizard made a plan. First he dug a deep hole, far into the ground. Then he plastered mud around the top to make the hole look small. When he was through, the opening was no bigger than a man's hand.

The lizard made another thing. He made a cape of flies. He sat before his house catching the blue and green flies that alighted, and with fine threads he wove them into a beautiful cloth. When it was finished, the cape was like nothing that had ever been seen in the country. Whenever the cape was moved a little, the flies buzzed and made a lovely musical sound.

Abosom put the cape on and went through the market place of the village. Everyone who saw the cape and heard it buzz wanted to buy it. But the lizard said: "This is all that I have left. My crops and my farm are gone. This is all I own. Why should I sell it?" They offered him many things in exchange, but he refused.

Word came to Anansi about the cape, and he went to the market place to see it. He said to himself: "I will buy this cape. Such elegance is only for me." That night he went to lizard's house, saying: "How much will you take for your cloth of flies?"

Abosom replied: "Since you have outwitted me and taken all my food, I am hungry. I will give you the cape if you will fill up the small hole in my yard with yams and okra."

Anansi went and looked at the hole. He said to himself: "The lizard is sillier than I imagined. I will give him back a few of his yams and get the cape." Then he said to Abosom: "It is a bargain. I will fill the hole, and you will give me the cloth of flies." They called on the chief to be witness to the deal. Then Anansi went home for the food.

He brought a small basket of yams and okra. He put the yams and okra into the hole, but it wasn't yet full. He went home for another basket, but when he emptied it, the hole still wasn't full. Many baskets were brought. Anansi's children were called upon to help. They carried the baskets full to the lizard's place, and they carried them back empty. Everything they brought went into the hole without filling it. They worked and carried all night. When morning came, the hole still wasn't full. Finally Anansi brought the last of the yams and okra and put them into the hole the lizarzd had made, and he cried out: "I have given everything! I have no more!"

The lizard looked into the hole, saying: "You haven't even begun to fill it."

But Anansi complained: "I have nothing more. My house is empty!"

"The chief is our witness," the lizard said. "You

promised to fill the hole. You haven't kept the bargain."

Anansi groaned in misery. But the lizard said: "I will discharge the debt if you return my garden to me."

Anansi cried: "It is yours; it is yours."

"It has been witnessed," Abosom said. "The land is mine. Here is the cloak."

The lizard took the cloak and put it forward for Anansi. Anansi took it and put it over his shoulders and was very proud. But just at that moment a strong wind came, and the flies buzzed, and before Anansi knew what was happening the cloak of flies flew away. Anansi ran after it through the bush country, but it was useless.

This is the way Abosom, the lizard, got back his garden and his crops.

Ever since then Anansi has been trying to make a cloak of flies like the one the lizard made. He spins his cloth and catches flies in it. For a while they buzz, but then Anansi gets hungry and eats them one at a time. And never has he been able to complete the cloak he is trying to make.

As for the lizard, whenever he remembers the false judgment of the chief that gave his farm to Anansi, he moves his head up and down helplessly, calling upon the Sky God to take note of this miscarriage of justice.

nansi Steals the Palm Wine

In the old days there was no such thing as debt among the people of Ashanti. No one owed money to anyone. But a stranger came to the country from the north, and this man brought debt with him. He owed money. The stranger cleared some land and made a farm. Then he cut down many palm trees and drained the juice from them to make wine. He put the juice in a large clay pot and left it there to ferment.

The stranger had to go on a journey to Accra. So that his palm wine wouldn't be disturbed in his absence, he decreed that whoever should drink this wine would take all his debts.

When he had gone, Anansi, the spider, came to the man's house and found no one there. He saw only the large pot of palm wine. Anansi put his finger in the wine and tasted it. It was good. So he drank. He drank a great deal, and soon he didn't know whether it was night or day. He simply fell and rolled on the ground.

When the stranger returned from Accra, he saw Anansi rolling on the ground in foolish delight. The palm wine was gone. Never had one person drunk so much palm wine before. Ten trees had been tapped, and Anansi had drunk the juice of them all.

The stranger told him then: "It was said that whoever drank my palm wine would take my debt. You now have the debt."

So Anansi had the debt, and he didn't know how to get rid of it. He went back to his own farm and planted corn. He stood in the middle of his cornfield and announced: "This is Anansi's corn. Whoever steals it will take the debt."

The corn came up, and the ears came out. And one morning before the world became light, a crow came down and ate some of the corn. Anansi woke up and saw the crow eating there. He said: "Aha! Didn't you hear the decree? Now you have taken the debt."

Now the crow had the debt. The crow went to her nest in a tall avocado tree and laid three eggs. Then she announced: "Whoever breaks my eggs takes the debt." And she flew away.

A storm came up and shook the tree. A branch fell upon the nest and crushed the eggs. When the crow returned, she cried out: "The avocado tree has broken my eggs! The tree has taken the debt!" The tree then declared: "Whoever steals my fruit takes over the debt."

It happened that the monkey came along. He

climbed into the avocado tree and tasted its fruit. The tree cried out: "Aha! You have taken the debt!"

So now the monkey had the debt. He didn't know what to do with it. At last he decreed: "Whoever eats my meat takes the debt." He went through the forest, swinging from tree to tree. And as he went this way, he lost his hold and fell to the ground right where the wild boar was passing. The boar leaped upon him and bit him. The monkey called out: "You have tasted my meat; therefore, you have taken on the debt!"

Now the boar had the debt. He said: "So is it with me as it was with the monkey. Whoever tastes my meat will take over the debt."

At this moment a hunter came to where the boar was, and *tao!* he fired his weapon. He killed the boar and took him to the village. He cut the meat into many pieces and shared it with all of the people. In the whole village there wasn't one person who didn't eat the meat of the boar.

Then Anansi came to them, saying: "You have violated the decree of the boar by eating him, and you are all now burdened with debt."

Thus debt came among the people of Ashanti. Some have it and some do not. Men spend their lives trying to get rid of it. And when one has it, his whole family joins to help him send debt elsewhere. And those who do not have it, they spend their lives trying to avoid getting it. Debt is passed from one person to another endlessly, and for all this Anansi is responsible.

The Elephant's Tail

Once in Ashanti there was a man named Kofi, who wanted to marry the daughter of a great chief. Kofi already had one wife, but he wanted to take the chief's daughter as his second. There were many young men who wanted the chief's daughter, and her father couldn't make up his mind which of them should have her.

Then one day the chief's wife died. He called all the young men to his house. His stool was brought out, and he sat under the tree where he gave judgments. He announced that his wife had died, and he asked the men: "What kind of burial is fitting for the mother of the girl you wish to marry?"

Many of the men were silent, for they could think of nothing to say. But one spoke up, saying: "She should be buried in a coffin of aromatic wood." Another said: "Her body should be wrapped in cloth woven with gold." Others spoke, too, each in his turn. When the chief turned his eyes on Kofi, Kofi said: "She should be buried in a coffin made of the tail of the Queen of All Elephants."

The chief replied to Kofi: "Very well, I have heard. Bring me the tail of the Queen of All Elephants, and you shall have my daughter."

Kofi went to his house and took his weapons from the rafters. He took his spear, and he took his knife. His wife said. "Where are you going?"

And Kofi replied: "I am going for the tail of the Queen of All Elephants. When I bring it back, I will get the chief's daughter for my second wife."

His first wife was angry when she heard this. Kofi went away into the bush.

But he didn't know where the Queen of All Elephants lived. He went this way and that, but no one could tell him what he wanted to know. Then one day he met a sorcerer on the trail. He asked him: "Wherever will I find the Queen of All Elephants?" The sorcerer sat on the ground and made marks in the dust with his fingers. He threw cowrie shells on the ground and watched how they fell. He threw them seven times. At last he said:

"Go this way to the north, and that way to the west; go past the Town of the Dead, and beyond, and you will find the place of the Queen of All Elephants."

Kofi thanked him and paid him with a gold ring. The sorcerer said: "Here is a juju to help you." He tied the medicine bundle on Kofi's arm above the elbow. He opened his basket and took out four eggs. He gave them to Kofi, saying: "These eggs are powerful magic. Use them when you are in great danger."

Kofi went the way he had been directed. He went this way to the north, and that way to the west, and he passed the Town of the Dead without entering. At last he came to the elephant village.

Around the village was a fence of pointed stakes, and at the gate was a watchman. Kofi asked to enter the village, but the watchman refused, saying: "Why should you enter?"

"I need the tail of the Queen of All Elephants," Kofi answered.

"If you enter, the great elephants will destroy you," the watchman said.

"I have to enter," Kofi replied.

They talked this way, and at last the watchman said:

"Wait then until they are asleep. Then you may enter. They sleep in a great circle, with the Queen of the Elephants in the center. You will have to walk on the elephants who surround her to get to the Queen. Walk firmly. If you walk lightly, they will awaken."

When it was dark and the elephants were asleep, Kofi entered. He walked on the elephants firmly, and they didn't wake up. He came to the center and saw the great Queen sleeping. He took his knife and cut off her tail. Then he went out of the village in haste so they shouldn't catch him.

When morning came, the elephants awoke. They discovered the Queen's tail had been taken, and they made a great outcry. They rushed out in pursuit. They found the tracks of Kofi's feet in the grass, and they followed. They caught sight of him, and they ran swiftly. They came closer and closer.

Kofi ran, carrying the great elephant tail, but the angry elephants were swifter than he. And when they were very close and about to seize him, Kofi called to the juju which the sorcerer had given him, saying: "What shall I do?"

And the juju replied: "Throw an egg behind you."

Kofi took one of his magic eggs and threw it on the

ground behind. It turned into a wide and mighty river. When the elephants came to its banks, they couldn't cross. But the Queen of All Elephants also had magic. She turned them all into crocodiles, and they swam to the other side.

Again they pursued Kofi. And once more when they were close upon him, he threw an egg behind him. Where the egg fell, there rose up a great mountain. The Queen of All Elephants still had magic. She turned herself and her friends into herons, which flew over the mountain. When they approached Kofi again for the third time, he threw another egg, and where it fell, there sprang up an impenetrable forest. And this time he left them behind.

He came to the village and brought the great elephant tail to the chief. The chief took it, saying: "This is indeed fitting for the burial of my wife. You will be my son-in-law."

So Kofi went home to his own house. He hung his weapons on the wall. He hung his juju on the wall. Afterwards he went out into the fields to see to his crops and to burn the dead grass.

Then he heard a great commotion; he saw a cloud of dust; and he saw the elephants coming. He shouted to his wife to bring his juju. She went to the house and brought it. But the elephants came faster than she. And just as they were about to seize him, Kofi shouted to his wife: "Throw me my juju!"

But she was angry with him for preparing to marry a second wife. She threw his juju into the fire.

Kofi felt the breath of the elephants upon him. He cried out to his juju: "What shall I do?"

His juju replied: "Turn into a hawk."

Kofi threw his fourth egg on the ground and turned into a hawk. He soared high in the air, and the elephants couldn't reach him.

In time, the great elephants went away. But Kofi was still a hawk. He called on his juju again and again for help, but it couldn't help him, because it had been consumed in the fire.

So it is that Akroma, the hawk, circles and hovers over a fire in the fields. He can never resist it, for it is really Kofi still waiting for his juju to tell him what to do.

The Porcupine's Hoe

In the beginning there was only one hoe in the world, and men worked their fields with a bush knife. For the coming of the hoe to Ashanti, Kotoko, the porcupine, is responsible, and Anansi, the spider, also played his part.

It is said that Kotoko and Anansi joined together to begin a new farm. When it was Anansi's turn to work, he took his family and went into the field and dug the earth with his bush knife. And when it was Kotoko's turn, he came to the field with a hoe.

He raised his hoe and struck it on the earth, singing:

"Give me a hand, hoe of Kotoko, give me a hand!
It is hot in the sun!"

The hoe leapt from Kotoko's hands and began to work in the field by itself. It cut up the earth over a great distance, and when night came, the porcupine said other words, and the hoe came to rest. When he went home, Kotoko took the hoe and hid it in his house.

But Kwaku Anansi, when he saw how the hoe labored, said: "Why do I break my back? I shall get this hoe and let it work for me."

So early in the day, before the light came, Anansi went to Kotoko's house and stole the hoe from where it was hidden. He took it out to the field. He struck it on the earth and sang:

"Give me a hand, hoe of Kotoko, give me a hand!
It is hot in the sun!"

The hoe began to work. It turned and cultivated the earth while Anansi sat in the shade and rested. Anansi said: "Whoever had a thing like this before?"

The hoe moved across the field. All the earth was newly turned. Anansi was satisfied. He said to the hoe: "Stop now; the field is done." But the hoe didn't stop, because Anansi didn't know the right word. It went right on hoeing. It hoed itself into the dense brush, and still Anansi couldn't stop it. It hoed itself to the edge of the sea, and still it would not stop. It went across the sea and came to the Country of the White People.

And there the people liked it and fashioned other hoes after it. And when they had made many, they brought some of them across the sea to the Ashanti people. Thus today among the Ashanti there are many, many of these hoes, and men use them instead of the bush knife when they have to till the earth.

The Sword That Fought by Itself

There once was a famine, and the only food in the land was in the storehouse of Nyame, the Sky God. Nyame let it be known that he wanted an agent to sell his food supplies to the people. Many creatures went to Nyame's house, thinking to become his agent. But the Sky God told them there was one condition: whoever was appointed as agent would have to agree to have his head shaved, so that everyone would know he was Nyame's servant. No one wanted to submit to this, until Anansi came along. Anansi told the Sky God that he would allow his head to be shaved, and so Nyame made him his official seller of food.

Nyame's servants took Anansi and shaved his head. It hurt him, and when he went out among the people, they jeered at him. But he sold Nyame's food supplies, and the next day he went back for more. Again they took hold of Anansi and shaved his head. Again it hurt him, and again people jeered when they saw him. Every day Nyame's servants shaved Anansi, and at last he couldn't stand it any longer. He took a supply of food from Nyame's storehouse and ran away with it without permitting his head to be shaved. He fled into the bush. He came to the house of a woman named Aberewa, who had powerful magic. He offered her a share of his stolen food in return for her protection from Nyame, and she agreed.

But the Sky God had a herd of warrior cattle who could divine the whereabouts of any creature. Nyame ordered them to seek out the hiding place of Anansi and to bring him back to complete his contract. The warrior cattle sensed the whereabouts of Anansi, and they went into the bush country to get him. They came at last to the house of the woman Aberewa, and they declared: "The Sky God commands Anansi to return."

"He is not here," Aberewa said.

"He is here, and we will take him," the warrior cattle said.

But Aberewa was not called Aberewa for nothing. She had powerful magic. She had a long sharp sword which could fight by itself without anyone's holding it in his hand. When commanded to fight, the sword would fight. When commanded to stop, the sword would stop.

She took the sword from the house and commanded it: "Fight." It left her hand and went out to fight with

Nyame's warrior cattle. It killed all of them. Then she commanded: "Cool down!" And the sword came to rest.

Thus Anansi was saved. He continued to stay in Aberewa's house. One day Aberewa had to visit another village, and before going she asked Anansi to guard her place while she was away. He agreed. But when she was gone, he stole the powerful sword and fled back to the town of Nyame, the Sky God.

He said to the Sky God: "I broke my contract with you because I couldn't stand having my head shaved every day. But I have come back anyway, because I now have powerful medicine to protect you in case of war."

Nyame accepted Anansi's explanation and did not

molest him. Then one day there was trouble in the kingdom. An army came to attack Nyame's town and subdue the Sky God. Nyame ordered the horns blown and the drums beaten. His soldiers heard, and they came at once with their spears and their shields. But Nyame saw that the army of the enemy was larger. So he called on Anansi for help, saying: "Now where is the powerful medicine you have brought?"

Anansi took out the sword, and he commanded it: "Fight!" The sword left his hand and went out to attack the enemy just as they came to the gates of the town. It leaped here and there, cutting and stabbing, and they could do nothing about it. The enemy warriors fell everywhere. Some tried to flee, but the sword overtook them and cut them down. At last the

entire enemy army lay dead on the field.

Then Anansi called to the sword to stop. He said: "Stop!" But the sword didn't stop. He said: "Return!" But the sword didn't return. He said: "Rest!" But the sword didn't rest. Anansi had forgotten the words "Cool down" which Aberewa had used, and so the sword heard nothing.

Having no more of the enemy to kill, the sword turned on Nyame's warriors and began to slaughter them. Anansi shouted out commands of every kind, everything but the proper one, "Cool down." And so the sword heard nothing. It kept killing until all of Nyame's army was slain. At last there was no one left on the battlefield but Anansi. Then the sword came and killed Anansi, too.

There was no one left on the field to kill. So the sword stuck itself into the ground and changed itself into a plant called Tinni.

And even now, whenever anyone touches the Tinni plant, it will cut him and cause the blood to flow. That is because the words "Cool down" were forgotten when they should have been spoken.

Nyame's Well

It is said that once in the old days the frog was jeered at by other animals of the forest because he had no tail. He was deeply embarrassed, and he went to Nyame, the Sky God, to see if a tail could be given to him.

The Sky God listened to the frog's complaint, and after considering the problem he said:

"I have a special well which never goes dry. I need a caretaker for this well. If you will agree to be my caretaker, I will give you a tail."

The frog said to Nyame: "I will be caretaker. Give me the tail."

Nyame gave the frog a tail and sent him to the well, saying: "You are in charge. Keep my well clean, so that anyone who is thirsty will always be able to drink."

The frog went to the well and lived in it. His tail made him proud. It made him conceited.

Then one year there was a drought in the land. The rain didn't fall. The springs dried up. Only in Nyame's well was there water. And this made the frog foolish and unbearable. When there wasn't any water anywhere else, the animals went to Nyame and asked for something to drink. He told them to go to his well.

First the buffalo went to drink, and hearing him come, the frog sang out: "Who comes to muddy Nyame's well?"

The buffalo replied: "It is I."

The frog said: "Go away, there is no water here! The well is dry!"

The buffalo went away and was thirsty.

Then the sheep went to the well to drink. Hearing him approach, the frog sang out: "Who comes to muddy Nyame's well?"

The sheep replied: "It is I."

And the frog said to him: "Go away, there is no water here! The well is dry!"

So the sheep went away and was thirsty.

Many animals came in turn: the gazelle, the wild pig, the cow, the elephant, and all the others. And to each of them the frog gave the same answer: "Go away, there is no water here! The well is dry!"

At last there was widespread misery in the country. And when the news came to Nyame that the animals had nothing to drink, he himself went to his well to see what was the matter. The frog heard him coming, and he called out: "Who comes to muddy Nyame's well?"

Nyame replied sternly: "It is I."

And the frog answered, as was his habit: "Go away, there is no water here! The well is dry!"

When the Sky God heard this, he was angered. He came and took away the frog's tail and drove him out.

So it is now, as it has been ever since that day, that the frog has no tail. He goes wherever he can find water and lives there, remembering the days of his glory when he was the Sky God's watchman. But Nyame never lets the frog forget that he caused misery in the land. When frogs are first born they all have tails, but before they are grown the Sky God takes their tails away.

The Coming of the Yams

There were not always yams in Ashanti. In ancient times, it is said, there were none, and the people often found it hard to raise enough food to last them the year around.

But one day a traveler came through the country carrying a yam among his possessions. This yam was seen by an Ashanti named Abu. It made him think. "If we had this yam growing in our country, we would have something really worthwhile," Abu told his friends. "We wouldn't have to fear famine the way we do now." And Abu decided to search for yams so that his people could plant them.

He took his weapons and began his journey. He walked for many days. Everywhere he went, he asked people if they knew where he could find the country where the yams grew. Sometimes they told him it was this way; sometimes they told him it was the other way. It was a long journey. But at last he found it. He looked at the fields and saw yams growing every-where. He asked people where he would find the king, and they directed him. He went to the king's house and explained why he had come.

"In my country there are no yams," Abu said, "and the people are often hungry. If you could give me some yams to take back we could plant them, and there would be no more hunger."

The king listened and considered. He said: "I will think about it." And he had Abu put up and cared for in his guest house.

After several days, the king sent for Abu and said: "I would like to help your people, but when they are well fed and strong, they may think of going to war against their weaker neighbors."

"This would not happen," Abu said, "because my people are peaceful. And is it not true that people who are hungry may go to war to relieve their misery?"

"Still, if they are ambitious, I would be risking a great deal to help you," the king said. "However, if you will bring me a man from your tribe to live here as a hostage, I will give you the yams."

So Abu returned to Ashanti, and he went to his father's house and told him what he had learned. He said:

"Father, you have many sons. Send one of them as a hostage to the king of the yam country, and then we can have yams to feed the people."

But the father could not bring himself to send any of his sons into exile, and he refused. Abu went next to his brothers and told them of the offer of the king of the yam country. He asked them to send one of their sons as a hostage, but like their father they turned away and refused.

So in desperation Abu journeyed again to the yam country and told the king he couldn't find anyone to act as a hostage. The king was firm. He said: "Then I am sorry, but I can't give you the yams without security."

Abu returned home sadly, for he saw no solution. And when he came again to his village, he remembered his sister, who had only one son. He went to

her and told her the story. She said to Abu· "I have
only one son, and if he should go, I would have none."

Abu said: "Then we are lost. You are the last hope.
In many lands there are yams. Here there are none,
and the people are doomed to be hungry." His sister
listened while he told how yams would change the
life of the people. At last Abu's sister consented.

Then he returned to the king of the yam country
with his sister's son and gave him as a hostage. The
king took the boy into his own house, and he gave
Abu yams to take home in exchange.

When Abu came back to Ashanti, he gave the
people yams to plant, and they were glad. The yams
grew and were harvested, and there was plenty to

eat. The yam became the most important of all the crops grown in Ashanti.

As for Abu, he declared: "My father refused to send a son as hostage in exchange for the yams. Each of my brothers refused to send a son. Henceforth I will have nothing further to do with my father or my brothers. It was my sister who gave a son so that we might not go hungry. She will be honored. When I die, all of my property will be given to my nephew who lives in the yam country, for he is the one who made it possible for us to eat."

And so it was that when Abu died, his cattle and his land passed on not to his son or his brothers, but to his nephew, the child of his sister.

As for the people of Ashanti, they said: "Abu has done a great thing for us in bringing the yams to our country. We shall therefore do as Abu has done, in memory of his great deed."

And from that time onward, when a man died he left all he owned to his sister's son.

In honor of Abu, the Ashanti people now call the family by the name *abu-sua*, meaning "borrowed from Abu."

This is how it came about among the Ashanti people that boys inherit property not from their fathers but from their uncles.

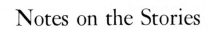

Notes on the Stories

Anansi, the spider, is the main trickster-hero of the Ashanti people of Ghana. Like the hare, the monkey, and the turtle in other parts of Africa, like Brer Rabbit in the United States, and like the mouse deer of Indonesia, Anansi's stock-in-trade is outwitting other creatures of the field and forest, even including, on occasion, the Sky God himself. All the folk tales of the Ashanti people are known as *Anansesem*—spider tales. The reason for this is "explained" in one of the stories in this book, "All Stories Belong to Anansi." Anansi is found, under various names, over a wide stretch of West Africa and as far away to the southeast as the Congo region. And when Africans came to populate regions of the New World, they brought their Anansi tales, among others, with them. Today you may hear stories about Anansi in many islands of the West Indies, in South America, and in the United States. In some of the islands he has become "Aunt Nancy" or "Sister Nancy." In Haiti many of his adventures have become the property of two characters known as Bouki and Ti Malice, with Ti Malice inheriting the largest share of Anansi's guile and Bouki taking a disproportionate share of his foolishness. Anansi's son Intikuma has also survived in New World folk tales. On the West Indian island of Montserrat he is called Brer Terycooma, and on Nevis he is known as Tacoma.

In nearly all of the Ashanti tales in which he appears, Anansi is portrayed as a creature without scruples. He outwits other animals most of the time, but now and then his unscrupulous deeds backfire, and he is punished. Often his actions exemplify how the small and physically weak may through shrewdness contrive to triumph over the strong. But there is no moral teaching implicit in most of his victories. While his shrewdness is applauded, his mischievous or wicked acts are not necessarily approved. Moral teachings are more likely to be drawn from his defeats. In tale after tale, Anansi is caught in some outrageous act and forced to hide his shame by disappearing into dark corners or into the tall grass. Anansi—and other animals as well—often do things that are wanton or vulgar, things that would be unacceptable in real life. In the framework of the folk tale, these acts may appear humorous to the African, even though in real life they would be grim and unpardonable. Thus the folk tale is not on the surface, at least, a mirror of Ashanti mores. Cultural values are so deeply ingrained that it isn't necessary to point out that this character is behaving badly, or that one well. The backdrop to all tales, unseen and unheard but ever present, is the intricate and delicate Ashanti system of values. When Anansi commits a crime, he commits it within a system which repudiates crime. If he gets away with it sometimes, well, that is a realistic conception. People who violate rules sometimes do get away with it. But sooner or later, in the next tale perhaps, Anansi gets his due. The *Anansesem* traditionally are told only after dark.* Usually the tales begin with a formula which stresses that they are not really true.

---

*One exception is during the daytime funeral of a person who was known as an exceptional storyteller.

The moral point of most of the stories is a rationalized one. For example, one tale tells why one should not give away sleeping-mat confidences; the reason stated for not doing it is not that it is "unethical," but because a great tragedy occurred once when such a confidence was violated. Likewise, another tale points the moral that if a brother or sister asks you to accompany him or her on a journey you should do it, because once when such a request was turned down evil things happened. Thus the basic moral values are masked behind "reasons."

While Anansi is always thought of as the spider, he often thinks and behaves as though he were a human being. The settings for the tales may be those of the animal world, of the human world, or they may be mixed. There are contradictions, which demand suspension of rigid concepts as to what Anansi looks like physically. In the gum-man story, for example, he strikes the effigy with his "right hand," his "left hand," his "right foot," and his "left foot," though a spider has no hands and a good many feet. The adventures of the spider in many cases might well be those of a human being. Rattray, an outstanding scholar in the field of Akan-Ashanti culture, believed that the animal cast was in many instances a disguise for human counterparts. Thus a wicked or ridiculous character in the community might be talked about indirectly under the name Anansi, while a rich man or a chief would be portrayed as the Sky God. Some who have tried to intellectualize the inconsistencies inherent in Anansi suggest the possibility that he may sometimes have a human rather than animal form. To the West African, at least, Anansi is *always* a spider, but he lives in a framework of human institutions and human values, and his wisdom, his foibles, and his follies are those of human beings. For the African listener, there are no contradictions and no problems in Anansi's character.

In the animal tales in particular, there is little stress

on the ordinary workaday vicissitudes of Ashanti life. One gets a glimpse here and there of such things as marital conflict. The story of "The Elephant's Tail" hinges on the resentment of a woman over the fact that her husband plans to take a second wife.

But one theme in particular reappears again and again —famine and the shortage of food. Many a tale begins: "There was once a famine in the land. . . ." Or in the middle of a tale the narrator says: "As there was a famine in the land. . . ." The basic food, the yam, plays a large part in Ashanti folklore. The tale which explains nephew inheritance, "The Coming of the Yams," tells how, before the yam became a basic crop, there was hunger in the land. Anansi's trick in "Anansi and the Elephant Exchange Knocks" depends on his shocking the community by wasting yams during a famine. In the gum-man story, "Anansi Plays Dead," the spider is motivated to his shameful trick by anxiety and greed during a famine. In the tale explaining why the elephant is small behind, "Anansi and the Elephant Go Hunting," the search for a non-existent yam garden is presented in a famine setting. Again, Anansi's connivance to get the lizard's farm has to do with the blight of his own crops. And in "The Sword That Fought By Itself," the story develops out of a situation in which, because of famine, only the Sky God has food stored away. The problem of drought is commented on in the tale "Nyame's Well."

Few opportunities are lost in Ashanti tales for explaining how things came about, whether the stories are about animals or humans. These explanations have to do with the physical appearance of animals, their habits, phenomena in nature, and so on. The Ashanti storyteller is alert to the need of commenting on how things began. Sometimes this is the focus of the story, sometimes it is casually parenthetical to the main theme.

All Stories Are Anansi's

This story provides the explanation of why Anansi is regarded as the owner of all tales that are told, whether Anansi appears in them or not. The pattern is characteristic of many West African stories, with the protagonist seeking a series of hard-to-get objects in exchange for some kind of prize. Another Ashanti version of this story provides a fourth test for Anansi, in which he has to capture for the Sky God a kind of "fairy" called *mmoatia*. To capture this creature, Anansi uses the gum-man trick, a device that is called on again and again. (See "Anansi Plays Dead.") Versions of this tale are known today in the West Indies, with Anansi still the main character, and in U.S. Negro lore. There is a proverb among the Ashanti related to Anansi's ownership of all tales: "Nobody tells stories to Intikuma." The implication, of course, is that Intikuma, Anansi's son, has heard them all from his father.

Anansi, the Oldest of Animals

This is a sort of humorous "tall tale." It caricatures the use of spurious logic to establish a point. Each animal utilizes some aspect of his appearance to prove he is the oldest. One interesting aspect is that the logic employed by the animals in the argument is just about the same device that the storyteller employs when he works backward from an observable phenomenon to a creative explanation. Here, with the animals themselves doing it, its weakness is satirized. The contest does not really establish Anansi's age, but merely demonstrates his argumentative ability. The humor of Anansi sitting on a nut shell, as a chief sits on a stool when in judgment, is immediately apparent to African children.

Anansi's Hat-Shaking Dance

Here is the explanation of why Anansi's head is bald, as well as why he is so frequently found in the tall grass, where he hides and spins. The foibles and vanities that are commented upon, however, belong to the world of real people. Anansi's invention of the "hat-shaking dance" is very funny from the African point of view. There is, of course, no such dance. The idea is simply an improvisation to explain why Anansi is pushing his hat around on his head. To an African child it is about as funny as an American boy's excuse, "I think my mother wants me," when presented with a difficult situation. The eight-day period that Anansi constantly cites constitutes the traditional mourning period of many West African peoples, as well as those of West African descent in various regions of the New World. The ultimate embarrassment that Anansi suffers when he is exposed in his hypocrisy is a serious thing. There are strong social pressures among West Africans for seemly conduct, manners, and ethical behavior. The public ridicule and contempt visited on violators are difficult to face; hence Anansi's flight into the tall grass. This story is based on a tale taken down by Rattray and published in *Akan-Ashanti Folk-Tales*, Oxford, 1930, and is used with the kind permission of The Clarendon Press.

Two Feasts for Anansi

Here we have an explanation of the spider's anatomy, and the moral lesson of what can come from gluttony and greed. Anansi is a perennial glutton. In countless tales he is motivated into some outrageous act by thoughts of eating.

Anansi Plays Dead

Once more we have an explanation of why the spider is found in certain places, in this instance in the dark corners of houses. As in "The Hat-Shaking Dance," Anansi hides out of shame. This story is the most common form in which the gum-man episode is presented among the Ashanti, although there are numerous variants. The gum-man ("tar-baby") tale is known throughout a large part of Africa and in New World communities settled by people of African descent. "Brer Rabbit and the Tar Baby" is one of the most familiar of U. S. Brer Rabbit stories. But tales with the gum-man theme have been noted in Europe and India as well, and an old version, involving a demon with matted (sticky) hair, appears in the ancient Jatakas. The theme is also found in the lore of certain North American Indians. It is interesting to observe that the precise sequence of Anansi's hitting with right hand, left hand, right foot, left foot, etc. (as with the demon in the Jatakas), has been preserved in the U. S. Brer Rabbit version, and that the accompanying comments are essentially the same. In the Ashanti version, the service held at Anansi's "grave" supplicating him for protection relates to widely held West African concepts of the dead as protectors and benefactors of the living. The irony of supplicating a "dead" Anansi for help while the living Anansi hides in the coffin is a source of real amusement to the African.

The Liars' Contest

This story explains why the spider eats moths, mosquitoes, and flies, and provides Anansi with a moral justification. Otherwise, it is a series of "tall tales" which delight African children. Anansi's particular aptitude for wily argument is graphically demonstrated, recalling his proof that he is the oldest of animals. Variants of this tale are known in Asia and Europe, though with a different setting and different chains of circumstances.

Why Wisdom Is Found Everywhere

Here again is the theme of Anansi's greed, as well as the resultant shame over his exposed ignorance in a situation where he had no excuse for ignorance. His anger appears to result from the fact that he has been embarrassed by a child, who presumably wouldn't be expected to know as much as an adult. "One head can't exchange ideas with itself" is the Ashanti equivalent of "Two heads are better than one." A more precise translation of the Ashanti proverb is: "One head never goes into consultation."

Osebo's Drum

This tale explains two natural phenomena—why the turtle has a hard shell and why the leopard has spots. And it again demonstrates the victory of the small and weak over the strong. The turtle's technique of persuading the powerful leopard to make himself helpless is similar to the methods Anansi uses to conquer the python, the leopard, and the hornets in "All Stories Are Anansi's."

Anansi and the Elephant Go Hunting

Here is an explanation of why the elephants live in the plains instead of the forests, and of why they are smaller behind than in front. The theme of forced dancing is well known in West African lore. There is another Ashanti tale about forced dancing in which Nyankonpon (Nyame), the Sky God, is the chief victim instead of the elephant. This variant has a parallel in a Haitian tale in which God sends the various saints down to earth to stop a big dance being given by a cult priest. One by one the saints go down and are overcome by the music. Finally God himself goes down, is "possessed" by a spirit, and joins the dance. An early prototype of this situation is found in the Old Testament (Samuel 1: 19). King Saul sends messengers to capture David where he is staying with the prophet Samuel; as the messengers arrive they find Samuel and his company "prophesying," and the messengers are overcome and also "prophesy." At last

Saul himself goes for David, but he too is overcome and falls to "prophesying" before the Lord.

The Planting Party

Among the Ashanti, as elsewhere in West Africa, the planting party is a traditional institution. Neighborly help with the fields is taken for granted, and community co-operation is the rule. This tale answers the question of what would happen if all of nature's enemies were gathered together in a common enterprise, and suggests caution. It also comments on hypocrisy, noting that one creature is shocked by the moral behavior of another only because he wishes to justify his own actions. And it further explains how the praying mantis came to have such a thin belly. The theme of one creature pursuing another in a chain of actions is well known elsewhere, particularly in Asia. For an Indonesian variant, see "How Confusion Came Among the Animals" in Courlander, *Kantchil's Lime Pit*, New York, Harcourt, Brace, 1950.

Okraman's Medicine

This tale is based on a story originally collected by Rattray *(Akan-Ashanti Folk-Tales)*, and is used with the permission of The Clarendon Press. It explains why the dog can never be cured of his thieving ways where food is concerned. He is not, however, portrayed as an amoral character like Anansi. The constant but losing struggle that Okraman wages against temptation makes him, if anything, sympathetic.

Anansi Borrows Money

Another tale depicting Anansi's amoral behavior in getting himself out of a difficulty. The trial-by-ordeal method of deciding guilt is not an invention of Anansi's. It has precedents in both African and European—and American

—life. The explanation is given here as to why a dying snake turns over on its back.

Anansi's Rescue from the River

This is a form of the riddle tale that is widely known throughout West and Central Africa. In most of these riddles of "who should get the prize," the controversy remains unresolved, and those who listen to the narration argue among themselves as to who should win. In one variant a man is saved by his three wives, and the question is posed as to which wife should get the credit. Usually the tale is left hanging there. One Ashanti riddle tale tells about three brothers who want to marry the same girl. One has a magic mirror that permits him to see what is going on anywhere in the world; another has a magic hammock that flies instantaneously from one place to another; the third has the power to bring the dead back to life. The one with the mirror sees that the girl has died; the one with the hammock transports them all to her house; and the third one puts life back in her body. And again the question is posed: Which one deserves her most? Another version of the tale in which a resolution of the question is provided is found among the Jabo people of Liberia. (See Courlander and Herzog, *The Cow-tail Switch*, New York, Henry Holt, 1947.) In this present Ashanti tale, the unresolved argument among the sons results in the Sky God's taking the prize for himself, and explains a natural phenomenon.

Anansi and the Elephant Exchange Knocks

Here is a typical Anansi tale demonstrating the spider's ruthless guile and accounting for the presence of elephants "everywhere." In the more commonly heard variant, Anansi kills the elephant with his third knock, cuts the elephant meat into small bits, and scatters it in all directions—a typical Ashanti formula for explaining why a certain animal is found in many parts of the world. In the more common setting, Anansi doesn't throw the yams into the river but uses them as toilet paper at the latrine, thus showing an unmatched contempt for their worth.

How the Lizard Lost and Regained His Farm

This story explains two natural phenomena—why the lizard moves his head the way he does, and why the spider endlessly spins and captures flies. The tale is known in Togoland, with the rabbit and the guinea fowl as the chief characters—minus, however, some of the "how it began" explanations. In the Togoland version, too, the chief's misjudgment hinges on the fact that the guinea fowl doesn't make a path. (See Cardinall, *Tales Told In Togoland*, Oxford, 1931.) The cloak of flies likewise figures in tales known in various parts of West Africa.

Anansi Steals the Palm Wine

In this story lies the explanation of how people in Ashanti first came to owe money. As usual, Anansi has a hand in it. His intemperate thirst and his lack of principle in taking what belongs to another are ultimately responsible for the coming of debt. Numerous Ashanti tales tell of the beginnings of human institutions of this kind. One, for example, tells how the Sky God left his young daughter to be cared for by a man named Gold (Money). The man takes care of the girl for some years, but she is finally seduced by the python. When he discovers she is pregnant, he runs away, fearing Nyame's wrath. The Sky God comes for his daughter, and when he sees what has happened, he orders everyone to search for the guardian. So far they have not found him, and that is why everyone is looking for Gold (Money).

The Elephant's Tail

In its central theme—search for a treasure, pursuit, and escape by dropping magical objects—this story has a universal character, its counterparts being found in Europe and Asia. In the form in which it appears here, or in very similar versions, the tale is widely known in West Africa. The elephant's tail is a special African ingredient. In East Africa the hairs (or "tail feathers") of the elephant are believed to have magico-protective powers, and they are often used to make bracelets or anklets. In a large part of West Africa the tails of animals are used by chiefs as symbols of authority and by "medicine men" as part of their ritual paraphernalia. In this Ashanti tale we get a momentary insight into emotional factors in polygamy. While polygamy was in the past, at least, accepted as proper for those men who could afford it, the emotional distress of Kofi's first wife causes his downfall. A New World variant of the story is found in Guadaloupe, retaining the elephant tail as a prize and for the same purpose—to be used as a coffin. (See Elsie Clews Parsons, *Folk-Lore of the Antilles*, II, New York, American Folklore Society, 1936, p. 137.

The Porcupine's Hoe

This story reflects upon the beginnings of the imported European hoe in Ashanti, while noting that its prototype existed in the country long before. Many Ashanti tales are built around knowing the words to make a magical object work and not knowing the words to make it stop, recalling our own "The Sorcerer's Apprentice" and "Why the Sea Is Salty." In one Ashanti tale Anansi finds a pot that fills itself to the brim with food on being given the proper command. He hides the pot and eats well, while his children fare poorly. Eventually they find the pot and discover the word that produces the food. When Anansi learns of it, he is angry. He finds a magic stick.

When the correct word is uttered, the stick beats all who are present. It will stop only when the proper formula is spoken. He leaves it for the children, who are tricked into saying the word that makes the stick beat them. As they don't know the word to make it stop, they are badly thrashed. Since that time, the tale says, children are whipped when they misbehave. Anansi has a further adventure with a magic sword which fights and stops when the right words are given. (See "The Sword That Fought by Itself.")

The Sword That Fought by Itself

Here is explained the origin of a plant with a razor-edged leaf. In this tale Anansi is killed, but there are many stories telling of his end, and yet he continues to come back. There seems to be nothing permanent about Anansi's death.

Nyame's Well

This story neatly explains why the frog has no tail, and even disposes of the complication that tadpoles have tails before they mature. A similar tale is known in Haiti, and one U. S. Negro tale contains elements of the West African version.

The Coming of the Yams

Many of the stories of the Ashanti are semihistorical in character, and peopled with humans rather than animals. This is one of them. Like the animal tales, it explains how something came to be, but the logic is more reasonable in human terms.